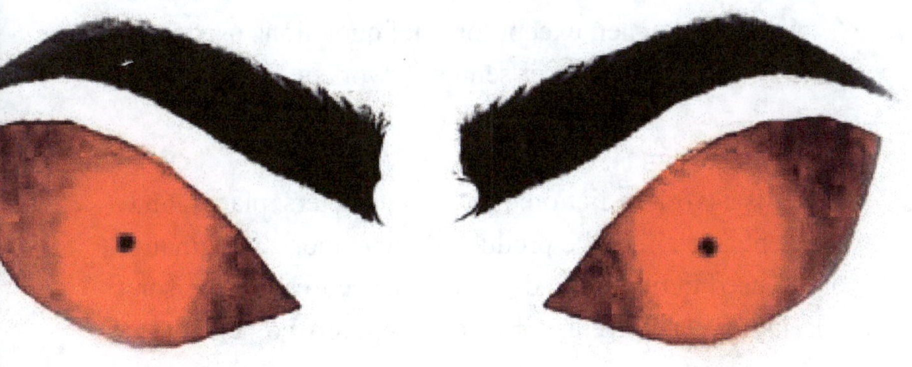

Demonic

By Val Keller

ISBN: 978-1-964283-97-5

Dedication

At a young age, you saw my potential — from writing small stories to scribbling words on paper, allowing my creativity to flow. To Mom and Dad, thank you both.

And to the man who pushed me every step of the way, making sure the book was perfectly executed — from editing and writing to even the illustrations — Alex Griffan from Woodbridge Publishers, I hope one day you see this book. Even though I can't talk to you, you made the entire process so much easier. I miss the talks we had and the moments we shared.

You are a dear friend of mine.

Acknowledgment

Special thanks to Stella from book writing founder's for reaching out to me about the book. she kept emailing me about the current state of the book. And the team behind the work of Book Writing Founder's for getting the book ready for publishing.

Table of Contents

About the Author

Valeriy Keller, born in Kyiv, Ukraine, hopes to see his future and passion for writing grow. He aspires to become a book writer. Follow and support Valeriy Keller as he embarks on a new journey of creativity.

Prologue

A chilly, misty morning in August of 1965. The haze tainted the air near Springfield Avenue, giving off a muddy, somewhat grungy feeling. The sun faded in the distant sky, spreading across the town with a yellowish glow, allowing one to recognize the telltale signs of the early morning. There were houses of different sizes, easily comparable to each other. Sitting parallel to each other.

However, somewhere hidden from the other homes was a tiny single-family house that sat directly in the middle. It was a peaceful, light shade of green. The surrounding area of grass and bushes was neatly kept, setting it apart—an ordinary home for an extraordinary family.

Tire's screeching, a sudden stop. The taxi driver announced in a raspy voice. "This is your destination, sir."

He adjusted his sight. Viewing the outside, his face nearly brushed against the glass, trying to recognize the street. He answered, "I hope so."

"May I help you with your luggage, Mr. Paul?"

"No, that won't be necessary, I only brought this suitcase."

"Ok."

Digging into the pocket in his jacket, he pulled a one-dollar bill, then replied, "Thank you for the ride. I would like to give you this."

"Oh, thank you so much! Thank you," Grabbing Paul's hand, a firm shake. "May God bless you," Paul replied with ease. Grabbing his luggage, he opened the door and hopped out of the car. Closing the door, I gaze at the scenery. The cold air brushes gently against his skin,

Violently shivering. Taking a step back, allowing enough room for the car to move. Watching it move away.

Unravelling the thick coat sleeve, he looked at the watch, reading Ten fifty-nine.

I hope this is the house. Please don't let me make a mistake. I can't fathom looking crazy.

He thought, pulling the coat sleeve back to its unwrinkled position. The grass is so green. The house is so petite. It was perfect. Even the small bushes scattered along the sides of the walkway were so particularly engaging. With a breath, he walked. Strolling from the road to the porch steps. Up the stairs. To the door. Pausing, he reached out his hand and knocked at the door.

The same knock on the door prompted a woman to run up and open it. Before opening the door, she thought, 'Who could possibly be at the door at 7 AM? Oh God, please don't let it be the William's Family!'

Of all the insanity in the world, it was nothing compared to the Williams'—very much like an itch that you couldn't get rid of. They were the absolute pinnacle of annoyance. Placing their noses in places where they shouldn't be.

They walked door-to-door and talked about God and the Lord to conjure up small talk just to get the information they wanted. As a Christian family, very much like theirs that attended Mass every Saturday, everyone knew the Williams family, which consisted of a mother who was a nurse, a father who worked in a small auto shop, and a son who attended elementary school. However, to Kristen's surprise, while peeking her head out, the Williamses weren't standing on her front porch. Rather, an older man with a beard is holding a black leather suitcase. She proceeded to open the door slightly.

"He... Hello... may I help you?" Kristen mumbled.

The man greeted her with an ever-so-fake smile.

"Hello, I'm Father Paul..." He paused for a moment. "Ehhhh, I'm looking for a woman named Kristen, or a man named Aiden? Am I at the right house?" the man asked her.

The woman's face, which once looked so peaceful and elegant to strangers and the outside world, now withered, frail in a frown, bruised, and devoid of the happiness that once shone on her.

Paul already came to sense within seconds by the looks on her face that she was either distressed, crestfallen, or in need of an exorcism, from the first impression. Some sort of abuse from a higher power was at play.

Hesitating, the woman covered her naked face with the door. Eyes bulging wide, she exhaled and offered, "Oh yes! Come in, Father Paul." She moved to the side to allow Paul enough room to pass through the hallway door. "How was the trip?" she continued.

"Very peaceful. Thank you for asking."

"Of course, here let me get your suitcase so you can take off your coat."

Just a step was needed. An unwelcoming presence had emerged. Shooting at him, nearly giving his heart out. Breathing became violent as he pressed his hand against his chest, trying to steady himself.

"Are you ok?" Kristen asked.

"Yes, I just... I just have to adjust myself from the car ride."

Telling a fib, extending the left arm, and giving the suitcase to Kristen. Then, he unravelled the coat.

It was difficult. Wavering hands trying to pull the sleeve.

"You know! They don't.... UUHHHHGGGG make these things easy." voice cracked under momentum. Finally, he undid the right sleeve, quickly pulling the coat off and setting it on the left forearm.

"Wow, that was difficult." He let out a huff.

Kristen let a smile watching him. Then asked,

"May I get you something to drink?"

"Yes, please! Coffee would be most suitable. Uhhhh and please, sugar." He smiled back, then cautiously proceeded with

"May I get my suitcase?" he asked, pushing his arm outward again.

"Ohhhh, yes here." She handed it back. Then stepped away.

Flickering a glance, the living room was tidy and clean. Astonished at the care, He whispered to himself: Not too shabby!

Two leather couches, sitting on opposite walls. Looking broken-in, the Indents' leather gave it an older, comfy look. Rather than tight new sight. Seeing around. Eyes were darting back to him.

In front of the couch was a small table with newspapers strewn about and a vintage-looking radio that did not play. However, nothing gave Paul the sense of belonging except for the view of huge photographs of children—one in a football outfit, and another in a cheerleading outfit.

Kristen nodded, her hazel green eyes meeting with Paul's. She then turned to face the couch of wondering eyes, disturbing the peace, loudly announcing, "Everyone! Father Paul is here."

The simple introduction sent everyone to their feet, and they glided over to the tiny hallway, where Kristen would then pivot, letting the others in for an introduction.

"Wow, Father, you're here early," a man said, wearing blue jeans and a polo shirt, with rough hair on his head. Paul noticed the eyes were so bright blue, with bags under them. They looked Dull. Wondering his eyes at the old timer. He seemed about in his forties. Spots of textured skin on his face that turned pale white, but were nothing more than a splotch or a pimple. Some scratches. The man gave a confused expression.

"Yes, yes! Do you want to know what the secret to my prompt arrival is?" With a pause, Paul looked at the man's uncertain eyes, then to each person with a smile.

"Priests have the right of passage to go through red lights if they are traveling for the protection of a patient, sort of like an ambulance or police car."

Suspicious faces looked blank -- looking without words. The man questioned, "You're being serious?"

"Of course, anything is possible when I'm not responsible. I'm not driving the car." He chuckled. The others did the same just to lighten the atmosphere. Everyone except Kristen, that was.

"Don't teach that to my daughter!" she spat, affronted.

Blank-faced. Eyes gliding down. For it was clear. The Photograph of the cheerleader girl was now visibly standing across from him. Eyes meeting Kristen's, he answered.

"I'm sure you have taught your daughter better than that, Ms. Kristen," Father Paul retorted smoothly.

"We're glad that you're safe. It's very nice to meet you, Paul. I'm Aiden," the Man changed the subject.

Reaching out his hand. Only for a polite gesture. A quick shake.

"Here is our daughter, Leslie." With a lunge forward, she thrust herself into his waist. Arms extended outward, wrapping around his stomach.

"Hi, it's nice to meet you!" the little girl exclaimed.

Blond, silky, curly hair brushed against his stomach. A delightful vanilla scent crept past his nose, immersing him in a time of his own childhood. Engulfed in the vision, he remembered the innocence of his youth.

A reassuring hug from a mother; the vanilla smell always kept him warm in trying and hard times. She would embrace him and offer words of encouragement.

"Paul, one day, when you grow up and your skin hangs and those eyes get lost, you will do the same for someone else. "Cause you will only have love left to give."

"I love you, Mom."

"I love you, too, Dear."

Was this what she meant? Was this the love she meant?

Pulling the so gently hands off, he lowered himself to her level. Resting the Suitcase on the floor. The Caribbean Sea was gazing back at him.

"Are you here for Keethen? ...Please don't hurt Him."

Paul looked confused, his ascending eyes upward to the girl's parents. They only looked back at him with deep concern.

"Keethen is her brother; he's the one we need help with," Mother explained in a deep sorrow.

"AGHHHH– okay."

Lowering his eyes, he reassured the daughter, "Your brother is in my hands; I will not let anything harm him."

It was clear. It felt like a truck was hitting him through his heart. With nothing to offer. But a suitcase. Yet, he still felt an aching pain when trying to speak.

Diamond, sparkly eyes took the words out of him – for he didn't see anger, sadness, or distraught. He only saw a lost child with eyes as deep as a body of water, but somehow also as blue as the sky, piercing him.

16

Eyes squinted intensely, a tear drawn down the rosy face. Nose stuffed. Sniffing under her breath, she asked softly,

"Promise? Promise that he'll…" Leslie's voice broke with the attempt to speak. "Promise me that he will be with me soon?"

Internally fighting himself to mask the fact that he was falling apart. In his kneeling position in front of the child, he didn't say a word – not even he realized that her words cut him so deeply.

Strength came easy to him. He usually would remind himself of that.

These are just clients, nothing more! Don't get caught up in their own doings.

However, he couldn't process what words to tell. Usually, it was a quick sentence, maybe two, but this time, it was like knives stabbing his vocal cords.

"Promise me!" she said more sternly.

"I…I promise."

Straightening up, back stiff. He hid his almost-shown tears. Then, he was approached by another man coming straight towards him with a hand outstretched.

"Hello, Father, I'm Reneled."

Which he shook.

Then, another hand came jabbing out to him. There was a whisper, "I'm Vetalie, very nice to meet you."

Father Paul observed both of their faces. Viewing Reneled as the shorter, heftier man. And Vetalie thinner, with a clean-shaved face, and much rougher facial features. Whereas Vetalie had much softer facial features, more bone structure, and a well-defined jawline.

Both seemed to be in their mid-thirties and professionally presented. Suits and ties.

"Very nice to meet both of you, Reneled, Vetalie. Aghhhh, so you two are troublemakers I keep hearing about?"

Vetalie jumped with a smile. "What? ...Trouble?"

Reneled added, "Ohh, I think he's talking about our water balloon fight." A smirk was added.

Paul's eyebrow raised. "You guys seem new? I've never seen your faces. I've just heard a lot about you two."

Reneled nodded. His face turned more worried, "Yes," he said, quickly gulping. "I'm new; I have only had two Exorcism cases."

Vetalie added, "I've been there for a while. Just never done an exorcism."

Those words stirred in Kristen's head. Her face became more twisted, she cried,

"The ministry is allowing two goofball priests to perform an exorcism without any experience!"

"Well, I have seen what they look like!" Reneled looked down, his face as red as a sunburn.

Her face narrowed. In shock. "Why would they allow this?"

Lifting a hand to Kristen, Paul replied, "Reneled and Vetalie will be accompanied by me. I have been through five exorcisms. When it comes down to it, I've had a great deal of practice."

After a moment of silence, he continued to inspect the area properly.

"His name is Keethen? And how old is he?"

"Keethan Ortaga, That's Right...And he's eight years old." Aiden responded. Then Kristen butted in

"He's been in bed. He might be sleeping."

"Very well, then." Paul nodded

"OH, How Silly! I almost forgot the coffee! Please, make yourselves at home. Come! Sit at the table," Kristen offered, smiling to herself after seeing everyone standing around uncomfortably.

Soon, everyone would stagger their way into the Kitchen. The fastest being the Young Leslie.

Paul, making his way through the TV room, asked, "Reneled, Vetalie, have either of you seen the patient yet?"

"No, not yet." They both answered.

Walked over to the kitchen while the others sat on various seats in the living room. Paul, being the last to sit, placed his coat over the chair. And the briefcase beside the chair.

He gazed forward, mouth pulled straight as a pencil, and his eyes opened. "Much better," he whispered l.

Kristen had begun banging on pots and pans under the kitchen sink.

"Are you alright, dear? You are making an awful lot of noise," Aiden yelled, facing his back towards the kitchen. Face scrunched.

"Yes, I'm OK! Just looking for the Percolator."

"OK! I was just worried."

Soon, the room became noiseless as pots stopped smashing and crashing. Paul would continue.

"Reneled, Vetalie, I want to put my trust in both of you? Do what I ask of you, and everything should go smoothly? Yes?"

"What if it doesn't?" Reneled voiced. "How do you know?"

Paul remembered the letter he received upon hearing this question. It was placed right by his couch, in the living room. In fact, having read it countless times, he remembered all the words.

Dear Father Paul,

After great lengths of examination, our church leaders and council have directed you with the task of our most recent case. Kristen and Aiden, a church family, declare their son, Keethen, in possession. We are asking you to carry out the accumulation of the evidence. Also, due to regulations, you will have to be accompanied by two other priests, Reneled and Vetalie. We believe in their ability to focus and their determination to work on this case with you. The case is from Tennessee, in the small town of Franklin. It's about an hour out of your way. We will pay for all expenses upon the moment of your acceptance of this case.

Thank you for everything you do, and more.

Council leader, Benedick Borsa.

"I perceive this family as a churchgoing family?"

With fixated, popping eyes and mouths open wide enough to capture a bug, Reneled and Vetalie stared at Paul. "What exactly does that have to do with anything?" Vetalie asked.

"Demons don't possess church families."

Aiden leaned back in the chair, readjusting to Paul's sarcastic humor. He found that it added to his confidence, abolishing his fear in return.

Don't worry, Keethen. We're coming... he pondered multiple times in his head with the same narrow face,

Both the priests agreed with an easy nod.

Much like the swiftness of lightning, the water started boiling over the stove. After a few moments had passed, she shut the stove off and poured the water into her coffee cup. Then, he crept over to Paul and gently placed the cup in front of him. "It's hot. Please don't burn your tongue."

"Thank you."

"You're welcome."

"What were you guys talking about?" Kristen had asked softly as she pulled the chair out and placed herself into the seat.

"We were getting to the point... may I ask you a couple of questions, Kristen, Aiden?" Paul stopped. He looked at Aiden and Kristen's faces, watching as the family came to terms with it.

Both parents nodded.

"How long has Keethan been acting differently?"

"About a year ago," Kristen said.

"Has your son ever been diagnosed with mental problems? Such as autism, schizophrenia, depression, anxiety, mental, or physical disorders? Anything I should know about?"

"No, why?" Aiden spat out.

"As a priest, in my knowledge, an exorcism can make the victim's health decrease and deteriorate with eternal damage, if not death, depending on the symptoms of their health conditions. Plus, the victim's health could be the reason for such acts to occur in the first place."

 Kristen replied, "Hold on, let me get the paperwork."

"No, that won't be necessary; your words are good enough," Paul told them.

"We must insist, so you know what you're dealing with," Aiden stepped in, watching Kristen leave her chair.

Her feet weighed down on the floor. Each step seemed heavier than the last. Her body shuffled, rocking back and forth with every step as she glided away.

They all sat in silence, with the exception of Paul, who was sipping his coffee. It was a long and uncomfortable silence.

"Here you go. Here's everything the psychiatrist gave us," Kristen said as handing Father Paul the files. His face distorted as he saw the size of the file, "Well, let's have a look." He whispered to himself, placing the glasses over his eyes.

"That's all the X-rays, brain scans, CAT scans… over the span of 6 months."

"Seems like nothing out of the unusual."

"Exactly! Which is crazy! This was when his episodes got worse," Aiden replied in confusion.

"Do you mind if I hold on to this document?"

"No! Go ahead, we have a copy."

Paul glanced over the papers. Eyes squinted, eyes opened. At some points, his beard would get in the way as he lowered his head over the files.

"He was placed on medication for depression," Paul stated, his eyes fixated on the papers, as he flipped through the pages.

"Yes. Well, my wife told them he had been saying he wanted to commit Suicide and slit his neck, so they placed him on antidepressants." Aiden watched Paul flip through pages.

"This other X-ray shows he had severe hand damage. What was the reason?" Sipping some of his coffee. "This was nine months ago, you guys went to a psychiatrist, a therapist-"

Aiden interrupted him, both his hands lying on the table. "The – the uhhh – he fell while having an explosive episode," Aiden said with difficulty.

"This has been going on for nine months?"

"Longer... it has gotten worse in the last month. He would make his fingers bleed and write on the walls with his blood."

"OH MY!" Paul discreetly looked at both parents in surprise, his head slanted slightly upwards.

Even Reneled and Vetalie were speechless.

Vetalie voiced out in anger, "Why didn't you tell the church earlier?"

"We just thought he was having problems with bullying, or perhaps behavioral problems," Kristen replied.

"The x-rays are clear; he doesn't seem to have any brain damage or even any kind of brain problems... can you guys tell me about his sports activities? I see that he was in some sports teams from the pictures you have up on the wall. Were there any football-related injuries?" Reneled asked.

"Oh yes, our family Pictures. Yes, but they were small injuries; cuts, bruises. Nothing too serious," Kristen replied.

"Any bullies or kids that picked on him?" Paul asked, stopping his sipping.

"No, most kids loved our son. They always greeted him with respect and love." Aiden folded his hands.

"He was popular," Leslie chipped in, taking a deep breath before continuing. "Everyone loved him. They all wanted to be his friend."

"How about outside of school?" Paul asked.

Leslie shook her head viciously in response.

"I see. I don't believe this family abused him, so I'll check that off the list," Father Paul said smoothly.

"OH, MY HEAVENS, NO! We love our children. He was always loved and cared for in our home," Kristen said, visibly distressed by the comment, her eyebrows narrowed downward while Aiden shook his head vigorously.

"I can tell. You seem to be very supportive of him and take care of him," Paul said, taking in a deep breath and keeping his head down at the papers in front of him.

"Vetalie, Reneled, you need to be prepared for this; If we are truly dealing with a possession, demons do not play nice." Paul paused, cutting himself off as he steadied himself by taking a moment to observe both of their faces, noting that no emotions engulfed their features. However, he could sense that internally, a shroud of fear was threatening to erupt around them.

"Things are going to happen. Whether it is scary or harmful, or just downright twisted, these are all tricks to lure you in," he eventually continued. "Don't get caught off guard," he warned.

"And what about the exorcism?" Reneled asked.

"Different demons are hurt from different exorcisms, which is why we must be careful. If the wrong kind of exorcism is performed, the child or patient can end up dying," Father Paul solemnly explained.

"First, we will weaken it. That's what the Holy Water and the Bible are used for. Once weakened, the demon shall come to forfeit itself with a name. Once we have that, we can do the exorcism." He took another sip of coffee. Steadily viewing the reactions from the rest of the table. Unsettling feelings overcame them; it was evident on their faces. Looking unsure of how to process the information.

The tensions seemed to be rising considerably, thick with dread, worry, and fierce anticipation.

Leslie piped in suddenly, sounding overwhelmed. "You promised my brother would be OK!" she exclaimed.

"He will be," Paul reassured softly, not wanting to overwhelm the younger girl.

Leslie cut him off angrily, "Then I don't want you touching my brother!" Her eyes glowed with a newfound rage; her eyes showed more concern.

Looked at her with the same calmness as before. "Do you want your brother to be healthy?"

"YES!"

"Then I give you my word that he will be," a hint of a smile on his face as his eyes met hers, driving in the sincerity of his promise.

With equal concern, Aiden asked, "How long does an exorcism last?" His eyes widened, hopeful with innocence and fear in equal measure.

Almost didn't want to tell him, but he could see that honesty was needed in this moment. "It could take anywhere between a week to five years... or more," he told them quietly in a raspy voice, followed by a cough.

Aiden's face froze, slowly turning white upon hearing this.

"Five years? That's insane!" Kristen murmured in shock.

Paul could see the restlessness in her eyes, which seemed to be consumed by hopelessness. "Not all exorcisms take that long," he explained slowly, "I'm just saying it could."

"Then how long will this one take?"

"Like I said, I'm not sure!" Paul's voice changed. It was deeper, more annoyed.

"Well, isn't there a way you could tell us… anything?" Kristen was growing annoyed.

The things I do for you, GOD… he thought in his mind, his hands resting on the table.

"There goes our family Christmas tradition," Aiden said sarcastically under his breath, his face distorted.

"I realize how hard this is on everyone, but we need to remain calm,"

"CAPEESH?" Paul reiterated.

Slowly and surely, each person on the table nodded in agreement.

"What room is your son in?" Reneled asked.

"He is in the room right down the hall, the one with the shut door," Kristen replied.

"Is anyone else in the room?"

"No," she murmured.

CHAPTER ONE

The war with death fought itself in Paul's eyes, swallowing away his confidence. It was only a matter of time until he found himself walking up the carpeted stairs, with Vetalie and Reneled following closely behind, feet dragging, hands and jaw clenching.

Paul prayed the Our Fathers and Hail Marys in his head. The overwhelming tension grew, making the air thicker with each breath. Every step cracked and creaked with the weight of the three priests. Feeling the walls closing over him, even with the assistance of the other two priests, Father Paul still felt alone. Coming to the top step, glancing down the hall. His eyes narrowed at the only door that was closed to the right. That must be the door. The only closed door… he thought to himself.

With hands sweaty from holding the briefcase, they glided down the hallway, the sun glazing through the window, sprinkling a soft light on the walls. The shadows of the three men briefly covered the light as they walked past. Goosebumps crept up their arms and legs, and soon all over their bodies. As they got closer to the door, they could feel the cold air around them, and they could see their breath as they released it from their mouths.

"Wha- what do we do when we get in there? What do we say?" Vetalie whispered. His voice cracked as he spoke; every word came out in a mumble.

"I'll do the talking," Father Paul insisted, his gaze determined as he looked at the door in front of them.

"What if it tries to hurt us?" Reneled asked next.

"It won't. Unless you hurt it," he paused his movement. He looked to his right, seeing Reneled inhale then exhale. "Ready?" he asked them, looking at them sternly.

"Not really!" Reneled breathed, shivering slightly from the sudden cold.

"Neither am I."

After standing outside the door for a few seconds, the three were completely silent. Paul eventually placed his cold hands onto the doorknob, grabbing the handle, but his fingers froze just from the touch.

OOOCH! Much too painful to open, he thought to himself.

With a twist of the doorknob, he pushed the door open. CRAAAACK! The door slowly creaked open.

Still standing outside, Vetalie called out, "Hello?... Keethen?"

A growl filled the room, followed by a child's voice, "Visitors? Hahaha. Who comes to me?"

The sound of chains moving echoed through the room. The bed against the back wall was faintly illuminated by a dim lamp, just enough of a glow to reveal a face but not to distinguish its features.

"Hello, Keethan. I'm Father Paul," he introduced himself, stepping inside slowly. "I'm sorry for intruding. I'd like to talk... There seem to be complications?"

"Father PAUL?" the voice growled, almost cheerfully. "I would LOVE to talk," it continued menacingly. "It's been a while since I've seen visitors."

The room was nothing out of the ordinary. Children's toys, a dresser with a lamp. A bench to sit on. But the sound of eerie laughter and unexplained voices filled the air.

It's all in your head, Paul.

"You mind if I sit?" Paul asked.

"Not at all, be my guest," came the reply.

Paul felt his feet grow heavy as he trudged to a bench. Placing the briefcase flat. And faced the shadowy figure.

Observed Keethan, he noticed red eyes with black pupils as small as grains of rice. Even unnatural for a human to have such eyes. Of course, one could have red veins in the eyes, not entirely red-eyed. Fingers long and pointed. Its teeth were as sharp as nails, all framed by ragged, greasy black hair and a distorted face.

This most certainly wasn't Keethan's facial features that he had seen from the Family Portrait. But the voice, OH that voice of a child.

Paul broke the silence, "Your sister Leslie misses you. She made me promise not to hurt you."

"Do you want to hurt me?" the demon intentionally asked out of the way for sympathy.

Paul ignored the question. "Why are you tormenting the family? Do you wish to kill them?"

"I would love for us to get to know each other. However, it seems you already know me," the demon responded. As silence fell again, their eyes locked in a tense stare.

The demon raised a hand, made a gesture, and then lowered it. "Now, may I introduce myself?"

"Sure."

"My name is Demonic."

"Demonic?" Paul repeated skeptically.

"Yes."

Paul laughed, dismissing the name.

"Do I amuse you?"

"Of course! You have such a way with words."

"Ah, and how did you think I would sound?" Demonic's voice softened.

"Raspy, deep… unforgiving?" it added softly. Silence enveloped them again.

"The point of life is for all species to be able to RELATE, LOVE, AND HAVE EMPATHY!" The demon paused, taking a breath. "The power to kill is enabled in all living things. You're reading too many fantasy books."

Paul's anger flared. He twisted violently to face the demon. "THE BIBLE ISN'T A FANTASY!"

The demon's eyes gleamed with excitement. He was getting what he wanted.

"Excuse me, I must pray."

"Our father who art in heaven, hallowed be thy name... I kingdom come... I will be done... On earth as it was in heaven-" Paul began, but the demon softly overlapped his words. "Give us this day our daily bread and forgive us our trespasses against us. Lead us not into temptation, but deliver us from evil." Paul whispered, "As it is in heaven, as now, and ever shall be, amen."

The demon echoed, "Amen."

"I'm sorry! I don't know what came over me."

"Apology accepted. Being alive... tends to make one realize how words can impact."

"What, particularly?" Paul interrogated.

"Words must fit with the overall quality of what I do. Be mindful, Paul, your life lies within my hands." It repositioned itself sitting up.

"Was that a threat?"

"No, it was a suggestion," It licked the outer part of the skin of the lips. "Does it help to pray?"

"It relaxes me," Paul admitted, scanning the room. He'd come to realize that no one else was present. The door was left empty. The feeling overwhelmed his brain. "Where are Vetalie and Reneled?"

"They're here."

"Where?"

"I think it's best for us to have some alone time… besides, peace that is disturbed might as well be no peace at all," the entity growled with a grungy smirk.

"Huh?" Paul looked Confused. He came once again to this realization: this was no joke, no huge GOTCHA! Moment. It was the real deal. "You're not hiding your powers."

"Of course not. If I wanted to hide, I wouldn't be here."

Paul, more terrified than before, sensed the danger around him. "Please, undo the curtains. I want you to see something." Demonic emphasized.

"Why?"

"Just trust me."

As asked, Paul undid the curtains behind the bench. Peeking outside, the world that was sunny was now snowing in a swirl of darkness. The houses in the neighborhood all had their lights out, and even the streetlights were off. Not a soul to be seen. Just dark and emptiness.

It was now evident and factually correct. This was an Entity at play. Even the most ancient experiences with exorcisms were never accompanied by evidence like this. Not even the boy Toby's exorcism was near this crystal clear.

"I don't understand?"

"Why do you think the doorknob was so cold?" The chains once more clanked and clunked. While repositioning its body.

"Have you ever heard of when Hell freezes?" Paul circled his head to the demon, "I have." Now chills ran down him. Freaking out wouldn't solve anything, but continuing the duties would. He gave out a Sigh.

"Do you mind if I take your temperature and heart rate?"

"Not at all," the demon spat out.

Moving the curtains back to their rightful place, he bent over to the Briefcase, Two CLICKS, a gentle push of fingers, and it opened.

"It's very nice of you."

"What is?" A flustered Paul is digging through the belongings. The leather of the case was extremely cold to his fingers.

Demonic replied, "To care for me," his eyes observing as the jittery hands removed the stethoscope and placed it around his neck. Then, grabbing the thermometer, "Mother must be proud of you."

It made a remark, but Paul did not buy it. Instead of slowly turning to face the monster, he walked over to the bed.

"My mother is always proud of what I do. Now, open your mouth," Paul instructed.

Closer inspection, Paul had a chilling glance at the hand. It only had three fingers and a thumb. However, the fourth finger wasn't cut off, but ripped. It simply did not exist.

The demon complied, spooning the end of it down its throat, dry lips curved around the Thermometer. With a hold, the thermometer beeped.

Taking it out of his mouth, he read the screen and then said, "Very good!"

"Indeed, ninety-eight is juuuuust right." Relaxing the thermometer on the sheets and picking up the metal edge of the Stethoscope.

Paul warned,

"The end of this might get cold," slowly demonic removed the bed sheets, showing his bare chest. The chains once more echoed. It allowed Paul to gently press the stethoscope on the bare chest.

"Please give me two deep breaths, then two regular breaths."

The breathing echoed soothingly in Paul's ears. The noise was nothing out of the ordinary. Everything was just right. Removed the stethoscope.

"Your heart rate is also good."

"AGHHH I'm healthy." It sarcastically, jokingly replied.

Paul walked back to the bench, shoveled the stuff back into the briefcase, not wasting time; he'd seen enough. "Well, I'll be on my way."

"Leaving already?" It quickly turned to face the baffled Paul.

"Yes, I must go,"

"But I'll be lonely!"

Lifting the luggage, he turned, both hands resting on the briefcase. "We'll play another day, but for now, you must rest."

"When will I see you again?"

"Some time in the future!"

"Alright, I'll be here waiting."

The conversation ended. Paul waited, but the demon remained silent. "How do I—"

"The way you entered is the way you exit."

"Thank you, friend!"

"Not a problem," It smiled as kindly towards Paul.

Without a word, Paul slowly made his way out the door. Slowly shutting the door. Seeing the outside sun against the wall gave him life again. He could also make out voices coming from downstairs. Moving as fast as a bolt of lightning, he scattered through the halls, down the stairs. He clutched the railing with his left hand and the Briefcase in his right hand. Voices could be heard fading as he got closer, until nothing could be heard but his feet. Walking past the Living room and into the kitchen. Eyes glanced at him.

"So, how did it go?" Vetalie asked, his mouth straight as a pencil, and his eyes looking at Paul with wonder.

"You want the lie, or the truth?" Paul replied sarcastically under his breath, "Allow the case to rest by his chair in the same position as before. Pushing the chair away from the table, ploughing himself down,

"It's not good," he whispered while pushing himself in.

"W-What's not good?" Leslie asked, her voice cracking, face frozen in fear.

"I uhhh-" his hands firmly pressed against each other onto the table. He shook himself out of confusion and started again. "Viewing the case from a professional standpoint... I believe it's best for the family to leave as a protocol of safety."

"Leave?" A surprised Kristen responded.

"Hold on, Paul! Nobody's leaving!" Reneled muttered.

"Throughout my time as a priest, I've witnessed stress, abuse, physical and emotional problems... By the looks of this, this is unlike anything I've ever witnessed... the patient's knowledge goes beyond natural comprehension; his manipulation tactics, most dauntingly, his powers that no human can possess. Kristen, Aiden, Leslie, I confirm, Keethan is possessed."

Blank faces and quiet mouths as mice, the family looked at him as if he were the Monster.

"No one is LEAVING! Father, you were there watching him play! You even told me; he's not possessed, don't you remember telling us that?" Reneled asked, looking baffled, throwing both arms out.

44

"RELAX! It was a manipulation tactic," Paul raised his voice.

"I STRONGLY DISAGREE! You were there, watching him... Vetalie, don't you remember?"

Sitting still and gazing down, Vetalie seemed utterly lost. His head was running in circles, and when he finally spoke, he did so looking anywhere but at Father Paul. "He's right."

"WHAT?" Reneled let out, angrily.

"He's right."

"HOW?!?"

"Remember, the demon uses control to-" Vetalie tried, but Reneled cut him off.

"You two can't be serious!" Reneled's face fumed, jaw clenching as he held in a deep breath. "This is crazy!"

Leslie placed her head down. Fearing an oncoming argument. "YOU'RE SCARING MY DAUGHTER!" Aiden snapped, taking back everyone's attention. "There is no need to fight, please-" he continued, looking to the table, his hands rubbing against his chin.

Paul took a moment to settle himself and process what he needed to say and do.

"I'll give everyone till this week to you're your belongings. I think it is best for the family to leave. just until the exorcism is over. Also, I'll be back tomorrow to take photographs and audio recordings. For evidence," he clarified. An unsteady breath escaped his lips as he gazed around the room.

"I will also write an acceptance letter with the documents you provided, informing the relevant authorities of the boy's possession. If all is accepted by the Bishop, December is when the exorcism should take place."

Tears formed in Leslie's eyes, and gradually, they fell, seeping into the corner of her mouth.

"I'm not going anywhere!" Her voice demanded. "That Entity upstairs is definitely not Keethan." He looked to Leslie, "I know deep down inside everyone misses Keethan, and I know how hard this is. But trust me. Staying here will do more harm than good. Go to a friend's house, a neighbour's house, or even your family's house. But staying here will be forbidden until Keethan is back in his rightful place."

"And what about school?" Aiden whispered.

"If you can give me the school's number, I will notify them of Keethan. And best for Leslie to keep going."

"It's ok, it's ok, everything will be ok," Paul soothed out his voice.

CHAPTER TWO

At one o'clock, the group agreed to have lunch at the bar. *The Merlot Bar.* A more modest place. It was a bigger joint than an average bar. In the dark corner of the dimly lit bar-restaurant, Paul sat with his hands down by his sides, waiting patiently. His eyes were more doubtful than ever while the thoughts played in his brain. The environment around him made him think back to the dark room. The atmosphere was thick with the lingering stench of cigarettes, and the echoing sounds of intoxicated humans singing songs, chitter-chattering, and a jukebox playing old tunes filled the bar. A haze of smoke hung like a veil, making it hard to see the various people.

"Something is troubling you, I can see it," Vetalie persisted, leaning forward in the booth, face partially illuminated by the overhead light.

"Me?" Paul raised an eyebrow, trying to mask his unease.

"Well, of course, something is troubling him. He's hungry. We have been sitting here for one hour and haven't gotten our food," Reneled responded.

Paul gave a faint smirk and turned his head to see Vetalie's reaction. "Reneled, you are a stick-figured man. You can't be eating that much."

"They didn't even give us bread. Are they trying to starve us?" Reneled persisted, shuffling himself over in his seat, his stomach growling audibly. "Ya, I can't lie. The service is BAD!"

Paul watched the scene around him with a mixture of emotions. A jukebox played an old rock song, and the patrons swayed, singing along with varying degrees of enthusiasm. The bar was filled with a motley crew of characters – from rowdy groups celebrating the end of the workweek to solitary figures nursing their drinks in quiet contemplation.

"They should make a rule: every hour we don't get food, we should get paid the employee's salary," Reneled suggested, voice dripping with sarcasm. Face turned and contorted with joy at the thought. "Do you know how well off we would be?" he exclaimed, chuckling.

Sitting in the booth, their eyes continued to dart around the room. The dim light cast long shadows, and the murmur of conversations blended into an indistinct hum. Their wait felt interminable, each passing minute stretching their patience thinner.

Paul's head swirled, stomach knotted, the walls around him seeming as if they would soon collapse. *Tell them. Tell them. You can't hide the truth forever.*

He could see himself in his mind, arguing back and forth, but outwardly he remained silent. Allowing the tension to stretch through dinner. Words were trapped behind a clenched jaw, and when they finally escaped, they came out cold and hollow: "Guys, I think we should go to the library." And once again, silence. They did as such. Now the three have been placed silently in the library, reading over books.

Reneled broke the quiet, his voice uneasy as they sat in the dim library. "Paul, I'm starting to get worried about you. You've barely said a word since dinner, and now we're here. Why the library?"

The stillness of the room was broken as Reneled shifted in his seat, brushing against the chair. Paul's face was drawn tight with concentration.

"Hol—hold on. I'm thinking."

Reneled sighed. "You've been thinking for two hours. We have been here since two forty-five the library closes in an hour; it's already five o'clock."

Vetalie, who had been leaning against a nearby shelf, chimed in. "He's right. We need to go home. I've got a family waiting for—"

"Shh! Just... wait," Paul snapped, cutting him off, his eyes locked on the script.

Reneled didn't back down this time. "I'm starting to think you don't actually know what you're doing."

Paul's voice dropped low, strained. "I know what I'm doing. Just... give me a second."

Paul's eyes scanned the dense, faded text, fingers tracing lines with an urgency barely masked by his calm demeanor. But after a fruitless few minutes, Renelled let out an exasperated sigh.

"You had plenty of seconds. You had *hours*," Renelled said, crossing his arms as he shot Paul a pointed look. He paused, brows furrowing. "You know what? I'm going home."

Paul glanced up, a flash of desperation in his eyes. "No! Just... give me more time."

"Time? Time!" Renelled scoffed, taking a step closer. "For someone who claimed he knew what he was doing, I'm pretty sure we wouldn't be sitting in a library, wasting 3 hours flipping through outdated scriptures on ancient beliefs." He spread his hands, voice rising enough to make the librarian look over her glasses. "So, tell me, Paul—do you, or do you not, know what you're doing?"

Paul glared at him, his stance defensive. "I know what I'm doing."

Reneled's voice rose, frustration giving way to anger. "Then what is it, Paul? Why are we going in circles? You're acting like you've got it all figured out, but every time I ask, you dodge the question. STOP HIDING!"

Paul crossed his arms, a hint of anger creeping into his tone. "I'm handling it, alright?"

Reneled threw his hands up in exasperation. "That's the problem, Paul! You're hiding something. Ever since the house, you have been quiet."

Paul snapped back, his patience wearing thin. "But I can't—"

Reneled stepped closer, cutting him off. "Can't what? Admit you're in over your head? Admit that you're scared? You've been leading us around in circles, acting like you have all the answers, but you're just as lost as the rest of us!"

Paul's lips pressed into a thin line, his gaze shifting to the floor. Silence hung between them, the weight of Reneled's words heavy in the air.

Hands squeezed his eyes. Paul sighed. "You're right. You're right." Then he lowered his hands to the table.

"Thank you." Reneled threw his hands out. Then proceeded to sit next to Vatelie.

"Look, something about Keethen's case is different. It's not like all the other exorcism I've performed. It said its name."

"Then why are we not performing an exorcism?" Vatelie looked with a scrunched face.

"First, we need the church's approval, as I stated before. And also, it gave me its name without me having to use the Bible or a cross. No demon gives away its name. It's like telling somebody your identity and they can use it against you."

Vatelie questioned, "And what is its name?"

"Its name is demonic. But that's just it…No, we're in biblical writing. Is there a Demonic? Lilith, Pazuzu, Baal, Abaddon, these are demon names. But Demonic is not one of them."

"Maybe it's playing with you. I mean, it could just be its way to lure you in."

"I thought that also Vatelie until its face looked dead serious. Just enough to be known."

Paul quietly whispered to himself, "It's not like Tobby."

***

My sacrifice, blood, and body are made for all. Form yourselves as a God. For a human going unwillingly from my word, will know the conditions of unforgiveness. If they see themselves as a greater god, then by all means do not lie. In the house, Liars are thieves.

Protect the image I have given you, for if you don't, the consequences are dire.

Narcissistic, Selfish, Powerful, no matter how they come, seeing above me will perish in a cruel underworld. Rise, for I have given you life, the greatest gift of all.

The man himself / Lucifer, is a temptation in my house. Sending millions of others wearing disguises to do his deeds.

Do not do him justice. Do not practice fakeness, do not lie, for you have already given him keys of heaven. I live in all of you. Amen!

***

The weight of responsibility was palpable, but Paul's faith remained unwavering. While cradling a rosary between his folded fingers, he lays his head low.

I am doing this for Leslie, I am doing this for Leslie, I am doing this for Leslie… His voice repeated.

His thoughts focused on the task at hand, arriving at the house with a renewed sense of purpose and a readiness to confront the darkness that awaited within its walls.

Paul found a fear much more significant. The fear twisted and turned. Shifting around his stomach, even displaying chills. Going to that house, up those stairs. Just the silence of the drive gave him nausea. Seeing humans and buildings pass, narrow roads of fall, and a colorful forest. The outside world was a stranger to him.

Exiting the taxi, Paul stood before the house, its facade seeming to loom larger than before. With a deep breath, he gathered his briefcase and approached the front door with measured determination. The morning sunlight cast a hopeful glow around him, a stark contrast to the shadowy presence he knew lurked within. A prayer on his lips would resolve his heart. Crossing the threshold, ready to face whatever awaited him inside.

Paul found himself once more knocking at the door, and once more having nothing to protect the people he loved other than words.

"Hello," Aiden's cracked voice mumbled while opening the door.

"Hello, I hope you are doing well," Paul replied, stepping inside as they exchanged handshakes.

"Yes, come in," Aiden whispered, motioning for Paul to follow him through the door. Inside, faint noises echoed in the hallway.

"Everyone is waiting in the kitchen," Aiden whispered.

"Who is it, dear?" Kristen's voice rang out sharply from the kitchen.

"Don't be alarmed, it's only Paul."

"May I take your coat?"

"Yes, please and thank you." Paul removed the coat, unwinking it and giving it to Aiden to take. They then proceeded to the kitchen.

In the kitchen, Paul was greeted with hellos, good mornings. He immediately noticed two unfamiliar faces in the room.

Before a word was thrown, Aiden intervened, "Paul, I want you to meet my sister, Chelsie, and her husband, Mike."

Chelsie and Mike stood up, Walked over to the side of the table. "Hi Paul, It-Its-It's nice to meet you."

Aiden noticed Paul's slight confusion and quickly added, "My sister has a stuttering problem."

"Don't mind her, she means well," Mike replied. He was tall, toned, muscular, with a sharp jaw structure, mustache, and brown hair. Chelsie, on the other hand, was a shorter side, and impeccably dressed with dark drown short hair.

 Paul asked, "Is it bad?"

Mike and Aiden exchanged a glance before Chelsie replied, "No, just some of my words get m-m-m-mixed up."

"It's very nice to meet both of you," Paul warmly greeted. warmly, shaking each hand. Mike, fidgeting with his fingers, asked, "Kristen called both of us, telling us you wanted them to leave urgently."

"Yes, that is correct."

"We are here to pick up their lug-," Mike paused, struggling for a moment after being pushed by a force. Glancing over to Leslie bumped into him.

"EXCUSE ME, MISSY! That's not nice, ssssssay you're sorry," Chelsie demanded.

Hearing that, Leslie stopped and turned, "Sorry Auntie, Sorry Uncle," she softly apologized. Head down before continuing on her way.

With a warm hug. Leslie looked up at Paul. "Hello, Father."

"Hello, Leslie." Paul chuckled warmly, more at ease now. "Oh, I got you something."

"What is it?" Leslie's eyes lit up with curiosity as she darted over to the nearby table, her feet moving quicker than lightning.

"It's a flower," Aiden whispered. "She picked it out yesterday."

"Aww, Aiden, you raised such a woman," Paul praised sincerely.

"Thank you, though sometimes, she can be over the top."

Chelsie chimed in with a half-played-off smile. "She's definitely a dad's girl," Chelsie suggested.

Leslie grabbed the flower from the table and rushed back to Paul, pushing past the adults with excitement.

She begged, "Ok, open your hands!"

Paul Bent over to her height. And she placed the small flower in his palms.

"Aww, Leslie, it's a Viola, how sweet of you," Paul exclaimed, touched by her gesture.

"Mhmmm, they come back every year in our garden. I picked it special just for you," Leslie explained proudly, wrapping his arms around her. The simple act of kindness meant the world to him. Their bond was unmatched.

"Thank you." He smiled.

To which he remembered the rosary he had tucked into his right pant pocket, he said, "I also got you something."

Shoving his hand into the pocket, he pulled out the rosary and gently placed it around her neck while saying, "It isn't much. But take it with you, it will protect you."

Leslie's face lit up even brighter, "Thanks, father."

The excitement had overcome Leslie's face. Spinning around to Dad's direction, she exclaimed, "Look, Dad, Paul gave me this. Isn't it just wonderful?" Fluttering fingers to the rosary, her innocent mind unaware of its significance but feeling its importance through Paul's gesture.

Chelsie pretended to be astonished, "You look so beautiful with it."

"Really, Auntie?"

"Yes, of course it reminds me of Mom," Chelsie suggested.

Aiden agreed, "Mom always loved Rosary beads. She used to tell us to pray the rosary once every day."

"So, as I was trying to say earlier, we are here to pick up the luggage. We might not see you after you get done." Mike Suggested. "Aiden and Kristen informed us about everything that happened."

"Very well then. It is nice to meet both of you." Paul confirmed.

"Ohhh My maners, Paul would you like something to drink again?" Kristen once again asked.

"Thank you for the offer, But No thank you. Im ok." He replied watching her eyes blink.

"So get this, Right? Yesterday they found leslies teacher's Son dead. It was on the local Radio." Kristen had sat down, Back hunched.

"What?" Chelsie drifted over to a empty chair. Sitting herself down. "Ya they picked the story up. Apparently, he died of extreme starvation."

"Who?" Vetalie looked to her. "her teacher's Son."

"He's a struggling painter."

Reneled being intrigued chimed in. "What is his name?"

"Ethan, last name Hayes."

The rise of a eye brow, being inpatient. With a glance to Kristen then everyone else. "I think we should start?"

everyone noded, responding "Yes."

Rolling up the sleeves, deep breath, more focused. Paul asked, "Kristen, Aiden, did anyone by any chance put chains on Keethen's hands?"

"Chains?"

Confusion and concern flashed across their faces. Aiden and Kristen both voiced together, "No," while Leslie shook her head violently.

"Why?" Kristen asked, her brow furrowing with worry.

"No, just asking… also, he only has four fingers? The tips of the fingers are sharp, Did any of you notice?"

"No… Not at all," Aiden voiced out, exchanging a puzzled glance with Kristen.

"Huhhh… Weird," Paul muttered, gathering his thoughts.

 "Reneled, can you grab my briefcase and just open it for me?"

"Yeah, I got you," Reneled responded promptly. Bending at the hips, extending the reach. His fingers curved around a handle. Lifting it in a weird position, he slammed it onto the table.

"How do I open it?"

"The two locks just push them up."

Flicking open the latch, he gently pushed up, viewing it open.

"What do you need?"

"Hand me the audio recorder and camera," Paul instructed, reaching for the items Reneled swiftly retrieved. As Reneled began to close the suitcase, Paul voiced out his concern.

"Also grab the Cross and the holy water in case anything happens, we have protection."

Reneled obeyed as told. Closing the case, he left it in the corner of the table. "I must provide evidence of Keethan's possession… I will be recording audio and taking photos. I also need everyone around the table to agree with me, furthering my experiment. Does everyone agree?"

Soft affirmations filled the room as each person nodded or murmured their consent.

"It can take two weeks to about a month for the church to accept or reject an exorcism. So, we are looking to be accepted anytime from Thanksgiving to the first week of December. CAPEESH?"

Once more, nods and quiet agreements echoed around the table. But what really had Paul emotional was the sight of Kristen grasping Leslie's hand, their fingers intertwined as they held tightly.

CHAPTER THREE

Like the first time the Priests ascended the creaky stairs, now they met with more dread as Paul led, with a firm grip on the rail. An unsettling cold breeze greeted them. Behind Paul, Reneled gently, cuffing the holy water, and Vetalie in the back, was gripping the camera and audio. The three made it down the narrow hallway, landing at the closed door.

Paul, circling around to face Reneled and Vetalie, breathes visible in the chilly air. He asked, "You're holding the holy water firm?"

"Yes," Reneled replied.

"Very good," he shivered slightly. "Hold onto it tightly. I'll instruct you when to use it."

"Okay."

"Do you want the camera and audio recorder?" Vetalie inquired.

"It would be best if you hold onto them for now, Vetalie," Paul decided. "We don't want to scare the demon. We want it to be comfortable. I'll take the cross. Barging in, taking photos, and audio is a horrible idea."

"I thought this was supposed to only take a couple of minutes?" Reneled gave a squinting look.

"Just do as I tell you," Paul instructed quietly.

"Ok," Reneled whispered back.

There was a swift knock at the door, and a snarl came from inside, "You're more than welcome in."

Paul pushed the door slowly and entered the room. "Hello friend," he greeted cautiously.

"Aghhhh… Paul! My friend," the demon replied excited.

"Hope all is good with you? Also, I have Vetalie and Reneled here. Do you mind if they come in?" Paul asked, hearing chains rattle again.

"Oh wow! Of course…The more the better," the demon responded with a widening grin, sitting up, fixing its gaze.

"You're not gonna make them disappear again, are you?"

The demon gave off a hideous laughter. "Only if you want me to."

As Reneled and Vetalie cautiously entered beside Paul, their faces dropped upon seeing Keethan. They stood quietly by Paul's side.

"It's splendid to meet you, Vatelie and Reneled. Come in, don't be shy. I don't bite." Its smile became more visible.

"So? What are we here for today?" the demon's eyes brushed back to Paul.

The lamp was still in the exact same spot. Nothing has changed since the last day they met. It gave Paul an uneasy feeling. Most children's rooms look different the next day since they play with toys or leave all their belongings all over the room. But here, nothing was different; it all stayed still.

Not allowing the thoughts to take too much from him, he voiced out, "May we capture photos and audio?"

"Photos? I love photos... Also, thanks for the cross necklace you gave Leslie."

"How did you know about that?" Vetalie demanded.

The demon chuckled softly. "My knowledge is beyond human."

Falling silent, the men hid behind Paul, like children hiding behind a parent for protection. They looked at each other suspiciously. Reneled had come to see what Paul had been telling them.

Approaching Vetalie, Paul took the camera and recorder. Handing the cross to Vetalie, "I would also like to ask you something."

"What's that?"

"How did you get here?" Paul queried, placing the recorder in a drawer.

"Ahhhhh… Hehehehe," underlining giggling. "I fell out of hell."

"No, I'm serious."

Suddenly, its voice deepened, "Do you believe I can piss rainbows and sunshine?"

"What?" Paul stared, perplexed.

"I can hear your thoughts. Please be open-minded. I understand that religion teaches you about the Ouija board. But that simply cannot happen. It's a game, not possible."

His eyes were attached, never leaving, not even separating from them.

"A board with an alphabet and numbers can't summon entities," Demonic snarled.

"Huh?" Vetalie murmured.

"If it were possible, school children would summon me every day with those alphabet name plates," the demon quipped.

SNAP... SNAP!

Demonic grinned as the camera shutter released, the shutter taking a few moments to print the picture. After a moment, he waved the developed photo, tucking it into his pocket.

"You know...I have something that's photo-worthy," the demon teased.

"What's that?" Paul asked, while looking through the viewfinder.

"Hold on," the demon replied excitedly.

The demon's hand slowly reached into the fabric sheets, pulling out what appeared to be the head of a child. Upon closer inspection of the deformed head, it looked like the head of Keethan Ortali. It was lifeless, its eyes blackened, and the neck was cut very neatly, as if by a guillotine. The sheets of the bed were clean; however, the head was a bloody mess. Demonic carefully used His powers to pull out the body from underneath the bed, exposing that the boy had been eaten alive. He raised the boy's head as the chains rattled and fell out of the sheets, squatting and extending it in glee.

The three priests stood paralyzed, each movement too perilous to attempt. Their mouths hung open, expressions of horror etched on their faces as they stared at each other in disbelief, their minds struggling to process the unfolding nightmare.

Vetalie, his voice quivering with shock, finally managed to word his astonishment, "How did… How did we not smell the blood?"

The entity laughed menacingly, relishing the chaos it had sown. "A-PAULed, are we? It's not like I'm the only one killing an innocent Child. For clarification, Tobby."

The words lingered into Pauls brain. locking eyes. The thought passed through the scrambled brain. Once more, back to his first exorcist. The realization crossed him like a bullet going past his eyes. The boy from his first possession and every possession he ever encountered.

The truth faced him. Trembling the knees

Heart full of bricks. Weighing him to the floor. quenching the cross tighter. He couldn't process what he'd done.

"You knew about it."

A smile plastered itself across Demonic's face, stretching to an unnatural size, its fiery eyes intensifying in brightness.

"You play no rules in heaven, so may you be condemned in HELL." Demonic paused. "You FUCKING SCUM!"

Vetalie, Reneled stood puzzled, face speechless.

"How did you know?" Paul scrambled on the floor. Face engulfed in red.

Demonic paused. Lifting a finger, "you believe that a cross, Holy water, and prayers will stop a human being strong enough to dismantle five billion people and the FUCKING planet itself... HA."

It stood straight up. Exposing himself. "PAUL, CONSIDER YOURSELF FUCKED!" The door that layed open, slammed shut.

Both preists cowardly stood behind Paul helplessly, processing the actions to take.

Only Milliseconds, it Took Dominance of Paul. Making him drop the camera. Smashing it into pieces. The lens removed itself from the body. Cracking the lenses glass. Without control Paul swiftly darted to rip the cross out of Vetalie's hands. Hovering the sharp edge of the cross to the forehead. kneeling before the entity. He Jabbed the edged point Making blood pour.

Keethan nude sprinted to the edge of the bed, leaped off, and aiming at Reneled, easily collapsed his weight to Reneled, kneeling on top. With fingers gripping the face, he shoved his thumbs into the eye sockets. Violently clawing his narrow, sharp claws into the eyes and Scattering the flesh and bones, dismembering his face as if digging for lost treasure.

"AAAAARRRRGHHHGHHAAAAAAAAHHHHHHHHH!!!!" Reneled yelled viciously. Yet muted. Words did not form, and sounds did not flow.

digging into the mouth. Blood stained the carpet, making a puddle. Vetalie quickly turned his body to the door, making a sprint to the door. But a force froze him before even a movement was made.

"No need for help. Everything is fine." A faint whisper. Then a trembling growl. Effectively levitating him to the ceiling, He'd become like a feather to the force pushing him. pinning his legs closed, and arms spread outward like a cross. pants unravled, and shirt vanished into nothing.

Paul unconscious, unaware of every moment.

Repeatedly jabbing the cross into the skull, piercing through the bone. The blood exploded as it now pierced the brain.

"THUMP!" was the noise, body hitting the ground. The blood splattered the entire room, staining windows, doors, and drawers. Demonic, hearing the body fall, swiftly vanished. The room was left silent for a millisecond.

"BOOM!" It reappeared. Kneeling over Paul. Ripping out the piles of flesh. One after the other. Vetalie, in horror, gagged to throw up, vomiting over Demonic's backside. The smell left an awfully stain on the blood.

Chewing the flesh, drinking the blood, and grinding the bones, "CRUNCH!" Incredibly, the Demonic's bone structure shifted and tweaked. Restructuring its posture and face, slowly mirroring words, stance, and even body. Lifting itself off its knees. And to a stand. Head slowly lifted, he spoke, "Have Mercy on me, Vetalie."

To copy the form. Only to watch the silence of him. It once more vanished, then reappeared in a squatting position, Allowing the weight to be distributed around Vetalie's legs. Without a claw or finger a incision was made. Collar bone down to pelvis. His shirt ripped open. The liver, guts, and bones exploded over Demonic's face.

"Come to daddy Bitch. Im gonna fuck you so hard you won't know where heaven is." IT Forcing him against will. Never dying but only feeling the ongoing torture.

CHAPTER FOUR

"It's been two hours. It's noon now, and they're not done? Maybe we should check on them?" Kristen's suspicions grew with every minute.

What if something bad happened? What if it doesn't go well…?

Ohhhh, Dear God, please keep my boy safe.

Her heart raced.

"They said not to interrupt. I think it's best we stay down here." Aiden looked over at Leslie with his hands folded over the table. "Hun?"

"Yes, Dad?" Leslie turned her head to face his direction.

"You realize this is a process. Right hun? It's going to take a couple of weeks. He's not gonna be the same right away."

"I understand, Dad. I just want him back. Back to the way that we used to be. I miss him."

Those words choked Aiden. Eyes teary, voice weak.

"We all do," Kristen replied in a sad frown. Still processing.

Aiden slowly shifted the chair back with a CREEEEECK!

"What are you doing?" Kristen questioned, looking across to him.

"Getting some water."

Kristen also stood up and walked to the kitchen next to Aiden.

A huge window above the counter was giving the room a morning kiss of yellow. It supplied an abundance of light, plastering rays onto Kristen's face. It showed her fair, crystal skin, almost clear enough to not notice her scars, scratches, pimples, or even blotchy displacment. Rays made her hazel, green eyes and curly strands of brown hair visible.

Her feet glided to Aiden, stopped beside him, and drooped her shaky arms around him. Gradually, the material of the clothing brushed his face.

"I know… I know. It's ok. You can cry." She insisted with sad, restless eyes.

A few wimps and then an interruption. All heads lifted to the ceiling.

"Someone is coming down." Aiden hid his feelings.

Finally, the silence broke. Footsteps bleed from upstairs to the kitchen. Kristen gradually unwrapped her arms from Aiden, walking to a pan on the stove.

"At least we hear something better than nothing," Kristen muttered.

"Must be Father Paul." Leslie slowly dropped her head, still having doubts. The boards creaked and cracked as feet could be heard making their way to the hallway and down the stairs. Then, from the living room into the kitchen.

"Hi Fathhhhhh…" Leslie swiftly blurted out, only to be silenced.

Everyone froze immediately, gazing with astonishment. To say the most, Keethen had made an entrance. Stopping at the kitchen, he scanned the area.

"Keethen?…" Aiden muttered under his closed mouth.

"Yaaaaaaa…? Why is everyone looking at me crazy?"

"Where is Father Paul? And the others?" Kristen asked, unable to move.

"They're cleaning up their stuff. They said I had the flu."

Kristen unconvincingly mumbled,

"The flu?"

"Ya, the flu." He paused, then started again. "Father Paul evaluated me. And I feel better now."

Kristen squinted her eyes with a head full of questions. *He's uninjured, not even a scratch on his face? No after effects of a flu, like sore throat, runny nose, or tiredness. What bullshit made-up answer is this.*

"Hey Leslie, wanna go outside?"

Darting eyes over to the table, she scrambled to get up delightedly. The wooden chair stuck to her as if someone had placed glue on the seat.

Kristen quickly intervened, "No, she doesn't."

With a couple of jerks of the chair, her voice turned worrisome. Placing her hands on the edge of each corner, she pushed herself out of the chair. Still, no effect.

"I can't get out of the chair?" Her voice was puzzled.

Keethen leaned against the wall of the kitchen.

Aiden stepped in, also being concerned, "No one believes you. That's a bullshit answer." Something seems off about you."

With a deep sigh, he answered, "Well, maybe something might still be bothering me."

"What's that?" Aiden stood firm.

"Well… I don't know!"

"Can someone help me? I can't get out of the chair." Leslie's voice was stern. She was bobbing side to side.

"Something just seems off…" Keethen explained. His form rearranged. Eyes turned to crystal blue. Hair became longer and blond. The face formed into Leslie's face. Size readjusted to smaller, copying exactly Leslie's features.

Both parents' eyes widened upon seeing this. More alert, Aiden turned to the cabinet, flinging it open by its knob and picking out a knife. He stepped out in front of Kristen.

"Who are you?" His voice was deeper and less raspy.

"I'm your daughter."

Becoming more terrified, her face scrunched, seeing a reflection of herself. "HELP ME!" Leslie burst out in a cry.

With distance, grappling with the kitchen knife, Aiden asked, "Who the fuck are you?" The tone was more serious. Not losing sight of the monster. A threat.

"I can't... I CAN'T MOVE!" in panic, she tried.

"Dad, I can't move. Can someone HELP ME?"

"I don't think it's a good idea to antagonize it."

Kristen hid behind Aiden for protection. Her mind was blank, body shaking.

"You're not welcome here," Aiden spoke, trying to see if it would help the situation.

"I never asked you. I'm welcomed cause your son welcomed me."

An uncomfortable laugh was emitted. In the blink of an eye, Aiden made a decision, lunging at it, with the knife outward.

"AIDEN!" Worrisome, Kristen screamed, only to view her husband freezing in midair.

"How about you drop the knife?" It smiled while forcing the fingers loose and allowing the knife to fall. Slowly dismorphing his hands behind his back.

"PLEASE!!! MOM HELP ME... PLEASEEEE MOOOMMM!!!." More desperate because of what her eyes were witnessing.

Frightened, mouth silent, and witnessing levitation, her mind couldn't keep up with the actions. Paralyzed by the fear, Kristen gulped and screamed, "LET HIM GOOOOO!"

Yet still traumatized, she helplessly watched. Aiden's shirt ripped open as his stomach exploded. Guts, liver covered, exploded through the ceiling. Paint stained with the stroke of red. Flesh hung from the ceiling fan, dripping off onto the floor. Numb from the pain. His rib cage was scattered on the floor.

"MOMMM...!!" Leslie called out in a stutter.

A smile was found slowly creeping around her mother's lips, Her emotions unnaturally gleamed. Lowering herself to sit on the floor, she picked up the knife. Circling around to Leslie, raising the knife with both hands, she whispered, "It's ok. Everything is great, HUN!"

"MOMMM!!"

dimples on her face, eyes glazing with delight. "HAHAHAHAHAHA! It's ok, baby. Here… I'll show you there's nothing to worry about."

Plunging the knife into her kidneys, rocking it back and forth, created an incision. The tender skin glowed red. Placing the knife into the left hand and crunching the left hand into a fist, jammed it into the incision. The sound of her rib cage breaking as she snapped her own bones.

"MOOOM!!! MMMOOOOMMMM!!!," Leslie placed her head down and shut her eyes.

This can't be real… This can't be real… NO! NOOOO!.

 voice cracked under pressure, and she cried at the gut-wrenching moment. It was so much for a four-year-old. Tears flooded.

Unable to run, she screamed for help. "PLEEEE… PLEASSSSSEEE MMMOOOOOMMMM." Her voice tone was strained.

Kristen, under the entity's control, was sloppily eating her own intestines. Chewing and munching through the cecum pouch. In the crease of her face, left pieces, she soon would lick off her corners in a disturbing, gross way. Tearing through the colic flexure, she devoured it like a sandwich.

"HAHAHAHA!!! Come on, Leslie! This is so much fun."

Leslie's heart gave out. body shut down, from the pressure and strain. head hitting the table. eyes closed from the stress. Breaths faded to a calm state.

Without words, Kristen was crunching and cracking into the testiness of flesh. Behind her, the entity slowly guided her, making its way to her, teeth ready to bite into her. The smile crested from cheek to cheek. Steadily increasing its mouth, biting into her neck, ripping pieces of flesh off.

Each part was more gruesome and gut-wrenching for Leslie to witness. It fed, chewed, and ate until only three bones remained.

The stench of it all soaked into the floorboards and ceiling. Leaving an ungrateful smell and soaking into clothes and leather. Unflattering, awful scent.

Here and there, the Entity would make her digest the flesh, shoving pieces down her throat. Till nothing was left. becoming unkept. Her body was thin enough to collapse. Yet it made her stay living, always feeling pain, exhaustion, and agony. For without the Entity's power, she would have been long dead. She ate the critters Rats, Possems, and natures animals, bugs that snuck their way into the house. Even digesting her own Fesses and drinking her own liquid urin.

Hair unformed. Her emotions and eyes hollowed. Always in perpetual pain. Without life in them, feeling every bite, flesh pulling, and blood sucking.

Soon she would also be left in death. Flesh rotting away from a recognized face of beauty to be dismembered in the chair. The entity's hunger for flesh, blood was its lust.

Days at a time, it would come lurking to feast on leftovers. Till nothing was left but stench and gut-wrenching odors.

The blood-stained walls gave a more brownish stain. Outside predators of the world crept inside to feast. Infesting the walls, counters, and hidden areas.

The house would rot to abandonment. Not a soul to witness its existence.

TO BE CONTINUED...

www.ingramcontent.com/pod-product-compliance
Lightning Source LLC
Chambersburg PA
CBHW071204300726
48975CB00004B/1287